This Walker book
belongs to:

Zander

For Mick
and in memory of my mum

First published 2013 by Walker Books Ltd
87 Vauxhall Walk, London SE11 5HJ

This edition published 2022

2 4 6 8 10 9 7 5 3 1

© 2013 Sheena Dempsey

The right of Sheena Dempsey to be identified as author/illustrator of this work
has been asserted in accordance with the Copyright, Designs and Patents Act 1988

This book has been typeset in Aunt Mildred

Printed in China

British Library Cataloguing in Publication Data:
a catalogue record for this book is available from the British Library

ISBN 978-1-5295-0867-3

www.walker.co.uk

BYE-BYE
BABY BROTHER!

Sheena Dempsey

WALKER BOOKS
AND SUBSIDIARIES
LONDON · BOSTON · SYDNEY · AUCKLAND

"What will we do now, Rory?" asked Ruby.

"I can't think of any more games to play."

Rory couldn't either,

he was feeling a bit sleepy.

"Maybe Mum will know one.

Let's go and find her!"

"Mum, will you come and play with us?"
Ruby asked. "We need a new game!"
"Oh Ruby, I'd love to," said Mum,
"but I just need to change
Oliver's nappy."

So Ruby tried some
hairdressing. Then she
put Rory in a lovely
blue jumper.

"Mr Rory, you are beautiful,"
she said. "Let's show Mum!"

Mum thought Rory looked very handsome but she was still too busy to play. "I just need to make Oliver's lunch," said Mum.

Grrrrrr...

So Ruby and Rory decided
to do some reading.
Rory was a very clever
dog but he couldn't do
all the funny voices,
not like Mum.

"Mum, is it time to play yet?"

"Almost ready," she said.

"Let me finish feeding Oliver."

Ruby stomped outside.

"It's not fair. Mum's always looking

after Oliver! Babies are so BORING!

If this stick was a magic wand ...

I would make that baby disappear!

FIZZ-WHIZZ-POW!!

RUBY'S AMAZING MAGIC SHOW

ROLL UP! ROLL UP!

Marvel at the Vanishing Baby Act!

Where: The Kitchen   When: After tea

Who: Ruby the Great and her Lovely Assistant,
Rory the Dog

"Or maybe ... when we go to
the supermarket, I could hide
Oliver in the cabbages.
Mum would never find him.

Woof!

"Or maybe I could sell Oliver
at the nearly new sale?
If we give him a good wash,
I bet someone will buy him."

Then Ruby had her best idea yet.
"I could build a rocket and send
Oliver to the MOON – *whoosh!*
Then he'd really disappear."

So Ruby began to build the Magic Disappearing
Space Rocket. And Rory was a big help.

"*There* you are Ruby! What's all this?" asked Mum.

"It's a rocket. I'm sending Oliver to the moon," said Ruby.

"It's a lovely rocket," said Mum, "but maybe Oliver is a bit small to drive it. Could we all go together?"

Ruby had a think.

"OK ..." she said, "but only
if I can be the captain."

"Of course you can,"
said Mum.

"LET'S GO!"

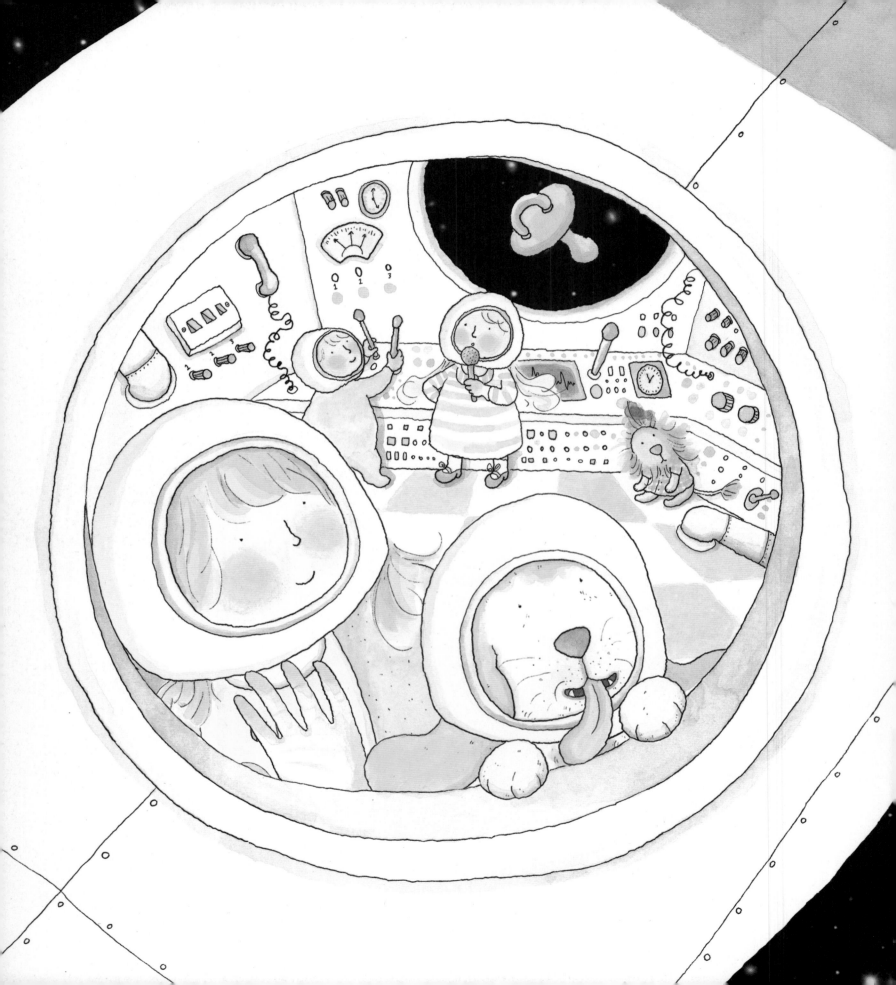

"THIS IS YOUR CAPTAIN
RUBY SPEAKING.
WE ARE ON OUR WAY
TO THE MOON.
PLEASE STRAP IN
YOUR BABY AND
HOLD ON TIGHT.
NO DRIBBLING ALLOWED."

It was the best space adventure they'd ever had
and they got back just in time for bed.
"Space travel is very tiring for
little astronauts," said Mum.
"Shall we get Oliver ready
for his afternoon nap?"

Woof!

And so they did.

It was time to curl up for a story and
Mum did all the funny voices,
just the way Ruby liked it.

"Mum," said Ruby, "guess what?"
"What?" said Mum.
"Today, I really wished Oliver
would disappear. But now ...
I think we should keep him a bit longer."

"Can we, Ruby?"
said Mum.
"I think Oliver
might like that."

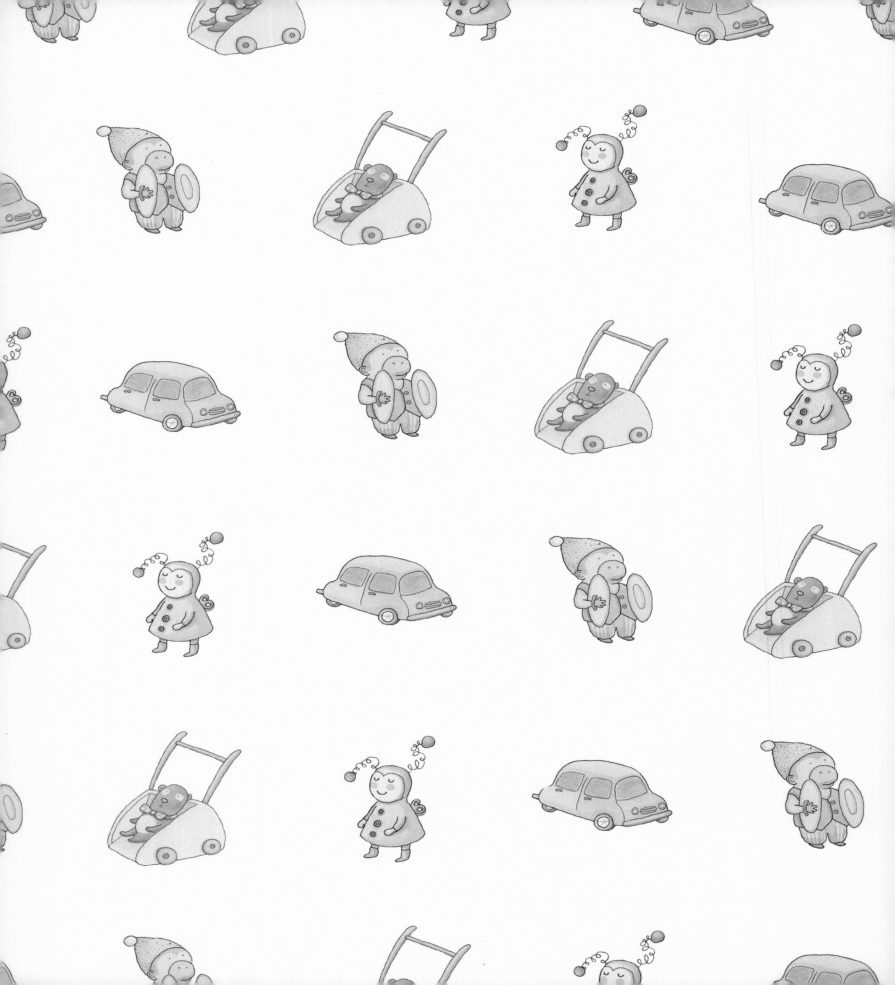

Sheena Dempsey

was born in Cork and studied fine art in Dublin
before moving to London in 2009. She graduated
from Kingston University with an MA in illustration
in 2010. *Bye-Bye Baby Brother!* is her first picture book.
She lives in London with her cute ex-racing greyhound,
Sandy, who follows Sheena everywhere and especially
loves watching her work in between naps
(Sandy's, not Sheena's).